'TIL THE COWS COME HOME

by Jodi Icenoggle

Illustrated by Normand Chartier

Boyds Mills Press

For Bryan,
Thank you for always believing.
The cows are headed home.
I love you
—J. I.

For fathers and their babies, especially mine
—N. C.

Text copyright © 2004 by Jodi Icenoggle
Illustrations copyright © 2004 by Normand Chartier
All rights reserved

Published by Boyds Mills Press
A Highlights Company
815 Church Street
Honesdale, Pennsylvania 18431
Printed in China
Visit our Web site at www.boydsmillspress.com

First edition, 2004
The text of this book is set in 15-point Stone Serif.

10 9 8 7 6 5 4 3 2 1

Publisher Cataloging-in-Publication Data (U.S.)

Icenoggle, Jodi.
    Til the cows come home / by Jodi Icenoggle ;
illustrated by Normand Chartier. —1st ed.
[32] p. : col. ill. ; cm.
Summary: A cowboy finds many uses for a piece
of leather in this Western retelling of a Jewish
folktale.
ISBN 1-56397-987-X
1. Cowboys -- Fiction. 2. Leather – Fiction.
I. Chartier, Normand, ill. II. Title
  [E] 21 PZ7.I235Ti 2004
2003108159

THERE ONCE WAS A YOUNG COWBOY who owned a ranch. He trailed his cows to the mountains in the spring and to the river in the winter.

In between his ranching chores, he made saddles and bridles and all sorts of riggins. Wranglers from miles around thought his leather poundin' was finer than frog's hair.

In appreciation of the cowboy's talent, an old
cowpuncher gave him a flawless piece of leather.
It was smooth as silk yet tough as a tornado.
The cowboy patted the leather gently every day.

At night he stared at the soft, cocoa-colored material and pictured a pair of chaps that would knock off your ten-gallon hat.

He measured. Yee-haw! He had just enough to make himself those chaps. Whistling, he cut out the pieces and stitched them together.

First thing the next morning, he took a quick stroll to check on the feel of them.

He wore those whoopi-ti-yi-yo chaps everywhere—
when he checked heifers, when he roped dogies for
branding, and when he rode his favorite horse.
    "I'll wear these chaps 'til the cows come home,"
said the cowboy to his horse.

After many rides through belly-high grass, a hole
wore in the bottom of one leg of his chaps. Feeling
flatter than a prairie pancake, the cowboy took them
off. He inspected the chaps. He had enough leather
for a trail-blazin' vest.

He hummed as he stitched it. He wore that vest everywhere—when he sawed his fiddle strings, when he pitched hay to the bulls, and when he dressed up for a two-steppin' shindig.

"I'll wear this vest 'til the cows come home," said the cowboy to his pardners.

After many a hoedown, the vest looked drab.
Feeling hornswoggled, the cowboy took off the vest
and began to fold it up. He discovered he could
make himself a rootin', tootin' pair of gloves.
He was sporting his gloves just in time
for a change in the weather.

He wore those gloves everywhere—
to fix fence, to muck out stalls, and to
go a-courtin' to see Sally Mae.

"I'll wear these gloves 'til the cows come
home," said the cowboy to his sweetheart.

After many dates with Sally Mae, his highfalutin gloves weren't so high any longer. Two of his fingers poked through the ends. Yet he still had enough leather to make himself a rip-snortin' hatband.

With two whoops and a holler, he patched together a hatband. He tied that hatband on his hat and wore it everywhere—to wrestle steers in rodeos, to shield his face from rain and sun, and to marry Sally Mae.

After many rain-soaked and sun-baked days with Sally Mae, his handsome hatband appeared old and frazzled. He slipped it off his hat and held it in his hands. He couldn't possibly save it now. Could he?

He needed a button for his jeans. He pieced together a jim-dandy button from the hatband and sewed it on his jeans. He wore those jeans, with his new button, everywhere. He wore them when he baled hay, he wore them when he broke his new horse, and he wore them when he held his baby girl for the first time.

"I'll wear this button 'til the cows come home," cooed the cowboy to his daughter.

After many rides with his daughter, the button
fell off. The cowboy searched, but feared the
button had fallen in the muddy corral. Now, this
cowboy knew he couldn't make a new leather
anything out of thin air.

So, he placed his daughter on his old horse and climbed into the saddle with her. As he told her the story of his flawless piece of leather, these two buckaroos rode to the pasture and brought the cows home.

Author's Note

'Til the Cows Come Home was inspired by an old Jewish folk
tale, known by many as "The Button Story." There are a number
of picture-book versions. When my sons were babies, I read this story
over and over, enjoying its simplicity and the message it conveyed. As a
person goes through life, what is accumulated is not the true value of that
life. Rather, it is what a person does with his or her life that matters.

I wanted to write my own version of the story, and an old Western phrase kept
running through my head: 'Til the cows come home. My story grew out of those
five words.

The cowboy is a universally known icon. So although this version of the tale is
unique to the American West in both its story and vernacular, I hope it will
appeal to people in different regions and cultures.

I hope you enjoy reading this story as much as I enjoyed adapting it. For those
unfamiliar with some of the words and phrases used in this story, I've included
the following jim dandy glossary.

— Jodi Icenoggle

Some Western Words and Phrases

Dogies — calves
Heifer — a young cow
Hornswoggled — tricked
Finer than frog's hair — excellent
Jim dandy — superb
Leather poundin' — refers to the act of making something out of leather
Prairie pancake — cowpie
Riggins — equipment that a cowboy might need
Sawing the fiddle — playing the fiddle
Shindig — a dance
'Til the cows come home — for a long time
Wrangler — another word for cowboy

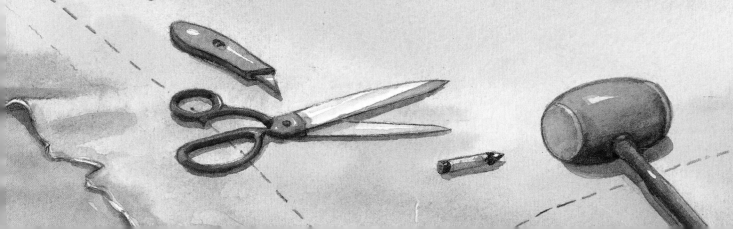